MW01049275

This edition published in 1993 by Mimosa Books, distributed by Outlet Book Company, Inc., a Random House Company, 40 Engelhard Avenue, Avenel, New Jersey 07001.

2 4 6 8 10 9 7 5 3 1

First published in 1993 by Grisewood & Dempsey Ltd.

ISBN 1 85698 523 7

Printed and bound in Italy

RUMPELSTILTSKIN
AND OTHER STORIES

MIMOSA
·BOOKS·

NEW YORK • AVENEL, NEW JERSEY

The Hare and the Tortoise

In the forest there was a clearing where all the animals gathered each evening after going to the river to drink. The tortoise was usually the last to arrive, and the other animals would laugh at him as he plodded into the clearing.

"Come on, Slowcoach," they would call out as he came through the grass toward them. The tortoise would blink at them and continue slowly on his way until he reached the spot where he wanted to settle down.

The liveliest of all the animals in the forest was the hare. He ran so fast that he was always the first to arrive at the clearing. "Just look at me," he was boasting one evening, "I can run faster than any of you."

The tortoise ambled into the clearing, last as usual. To everyone's surprise, he went slowly across to the hare.

"Since you run so fast, could you beat me in a race?" he asked.

"*I*, beat *you*, in a *race*!" exclaimed the hare, and he fell on the ground laughing. "Of course I would beat you. You name the distance, Tortoise, but don't make it too far for your short little legs," and he roared with laughter again.

Most of the other animals laughed too. It did seem a very comic idea. The fox said,

"Come on then, Tortoise, name the distance and the time and then we will all come to watch."

"Let us start tomorrow morning, at sunrise," suggested the tortoise. "We'll run from this clearing to the edge of the forest and return along the bank of the river to this spot again."

"Why, it will take you all day to go so far, Tortoise. Are you sure you want to go ahead with it?" asked the hare. He grinned at the thought of the easy victory he would have.

"I am sure," replied the tortoise. "The first one back to this clearing will be the winner."

"Agreed!" said the hare, as the tortoise settled down in some long grass to sleep for the night.

The next morning the clearing was full of animals who had come to see the start of the great race. Some ran along to the edge of the forest, others chose good places to watch along the way.

The hare and the tortoise stood side by side. As the sun rose, the fox called,

"Ready, steady, go!"

The hare jumped up and in no time at all he was far ahead of the tortoise, almost out of sight. The tortoise started off in the same direction. He plodded along, slowly picking up his feet, then slowly putting them down only a little in front of where they had been before.

"Come on, Tortoise," called his friends anxiously. But he did not lift up his foot to wave at them as the hare had done. He kept on moving slowly forward.

In a few minutes the hare was a long way from the starting line so he slowed down. "It's going to take the tortoise all day," he thought, "so there is no need for me to hurry." He stopped to talk to friends and nibble juicy grass here and there along the path.

By the time he reached halfway the sun was high in the sky and the day became very hot. The animals who were waiting there saw the hare turn back toward the clearing. They settled down for a long wait for the tortoise.

As he returned by the river, the hot sun and the grass he had eaten made the hare feel sleepy.

"There's no need to hurry," he told himself. "Here's a nice shady spot," and he stretched himself out comfortably on the ground. With paws beneath his head, he murmured sleepily, "It won't matter if Tortoise passes me, I'm much faster than he is. I'll still get back first and win the race." He drifted off to sleep.

Meanwhile the tortoise went on slowly. He reached the edge of the forest quite soon after the hare, for he had not stopped to talk to friends or eat tempting fresh grass. Before long, smiling gently, he passed the hare sleeping in the shade.

The animals in the clearing waited all day for the hare to return, but he did not arrive. The sun was setting before they saw the tortoise plodding toward them.

"Where is the hare?" they called out. The tortoise did not waste his breath in answering but came steadily toward them.

"Hurrah, Tortoise has won. Well done, Slowcoach!" the animals cheered.

Only when he knew he had won the race did Tortoise speak.

"Hare? Oh, he's asleep back there by the river."

There was a sudden flurry and at great speed the hare burst into the clearing. He had woken and, seeing how long the shadows were, realized he had slept for much longer than he intended. He raced back to the clearing but he was too late.

Tortoise smiled and said, "Slow and steady wins the race."

Rumpelstiltskin

One day a king was riding through a village in his kingdom when he heard a woman singing.

"My daughter has burned five cakes today.
My daughter has burned five cakes today."

It was the miller's wife who was cross with her daughter for being so careless. The king stopped to hear her song again. The miller's wife hoped to impress the king so she sang,

"My daughter has spun fine gold today,
My daughter has spun fine gold today."

And she boasted that her daughter could spin straw into gold.

The king was greatly impressed and said to the miller's wife,

"If your daughter will spin for me in my palace, I'll give her many presents. I might even make her my queen."

"What a wonderful opportunity," thought the miller's wife, and she fetched her daughter.

The king took the girl back to the palace. He ordered a spinning wheel to be placed in a room filled with straw.

"Spin this into gold by the morning or you will die," he commanded, and he locked her in.

The poor girl wept bitterly. For of course she could not spin

straw into gold as her mother had foolishly boasted.

Suddenly a little man appeared from nowhere.

"What will you give me, pretty girl, if I spin this straw into gold for you?" he asked.

"My necklace," said the girl.

The little man sat down by the spinning wheel. Singing strange songs, he spun all the straw into fine gold thread. Then he took the girl's necklace and, with a skip and a hop and a stamp of his foot, he disappeared .

When the king unlocked the room the next morning he was delighted to see the skeins of golden thread. But that evening he took the miller's daughter to another room with an even bigger pile of straw.

"Spin this into gold by the morning," he ordered, "or you will die." And out he went, locking the door behind him.

The poor girl stared at the straw and the spinning wheel. Suddenly the same little man stood before her.

"What will you give me this time if I spin your gold for you?"

"My bracelet," said the miller's daughter.

The little man set the spinning wheel whirring. Singing his strange songs, he quickly turned the straw into gold thread. By dawn he had finished and, snatching the bracelet, he disappeared with a skip and a hop and a stamp of his foot.

The king was delighted that morning, but still not satisfied. "If this girl can really spin gold from straw," he thought to himself greedily, "I shall always be rich if I make her my wife and keep her here. I shall try her once more."

So on the third night the king took the miller's daughter into another room with an even greater pile of straw.

"Spin this into gold," he commanded. "If you succeed, I shall marry you and you shall be queen. If you fail, I shall chop off your head." And out he went, locking the door behind him.

Once more, as the girl wept bitterly before the pile of straw and the spinning wheel, the little man appeared from nowhere.

"I see you need my help again," he said. "How will you reward me this time if I save your life?"

"I have nothing more to give you," the miller's daughter said in despair.

"Ah!" said the little man, "but if the straw is spun into gold tonight, you will become queen. Will you promise to give me your first child when it is born?"

"Yes! Yes!" cried the girl. She was sure that when this time came she could somehow save her child.

So the little man sat and twirled the spinning wheel, tap-tapping his foot on the floor and singing his strange songs. Then, with a skip and a hop and a stamp of his foot, he was gone.

The next day the king was delighted with the gold, and he made the miller's daughter his queen as he had promised.

And as queen the miller's daughter forgot all about her promise to the little man. About a year later, a fine son was born, and she was horrified when the little man appeared again.

"I have come to claim the child you promised me," he said, stamping his foot as he spoke.

"Take my jewels and all this gold," pleaded the queen, "only leave me my little son."

The little man thought for a moment and said, "Very well, I will give you three days in which to guess my name. You may have three guesses each night. If you fail, the baby is mine."

The queen sent for all her servants and asked them to go

throughout the kingdom asking if anyone had heard of the little man and if they knew his name. The first night the little man came the queen tried some unusual names.

"Is it Caspar?" she asked.

"No!" he said and stamped his foot in delight.

"Is it Balthazar?"

"No!" he said and stamped his foot again.

"Is it Melchior?"

"No!" he cried. He stamped his foot and disappeared.

The next evening the queen thought she would try some everyday names. So when the little man appeared she asked,

"Is your name John?"

"No!" he said with his usual stamp.

"Is it Michael?"

"Is it James?"

"No! No!" he cried, stamping his foot each time, and again he disappeared.

On the third and final day the queen was distraught for she could not see how she could guess the little man's name.

The palace servants came back without any news, all except for one who returned to the palace toward the end of the day. He went straight to the queen and told her that at the very edge of the kingdom, under the mountains, he had heard a little man singing this strange song as he danced around his fire:

"Today I brew, tomorrow I bake,
Next day the queen's child I'll take.
How glad I am that nobody knows
My name is Rumpelstiltskin."

The queen clapped her hands with joy and rewarded the servant for his discovery. That night the little man appeared and asked if she had guessed his name.

"Is it Ichabod?"

"No!" he cried with pleasure as he stamped his foot.

"Is it Carl?"

"No!" he shouted and stamped his foot with glee.

"Is it . . ." the queen hesitated. "Is it Rumpelstiltskin?"

Now it was the queen's turn to laugh. The little man stamped his foot so hard it went right through the floor and that was the end of Rumpelstiltskin.

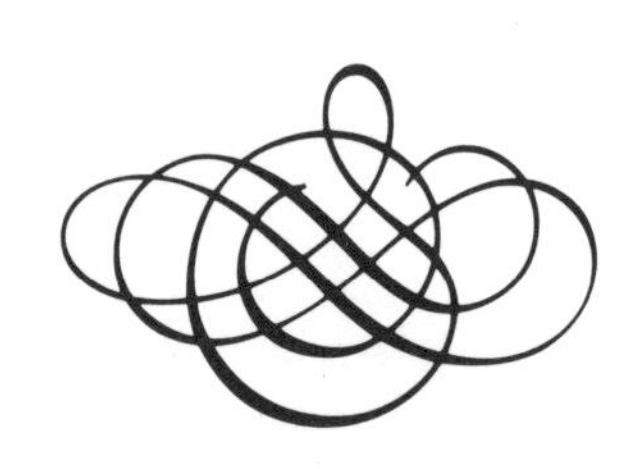

The Little House

Once upon a time a large earthenware jar rolled off the back of a cart that was going to market. It came to rest in the grass at the side of the road.

By and by a mouse came along and looked at the jar. "What a fine house that would make," he thought, and he called out:

"Little house, little house,
Who lives in the little house?"

Nobody answered so the mouse peeped in and saw that it was empty. He moved in straightaway and began to live there.

Before long a frog came along and saw the jar. "What a fine house that would make," he thought, and he called out:

"Little house, little house,
Who lives in the little house?"

and he heard:

"I, Mr. Mouse.
I live in the little house.
Who are you?"

"I am Mr. Frog," came the reply.

"Come in Mr. Frog, and we can live here together," called out the mouse.

So the mouse and the frog lived happily together in the little house. Then one day a hare came running along the road and saw the little house. He called out:

"Little house, little house,
Who lives in the little house?"

and he heard:

"Mr. Frog and Mr. Mouse,
We live in the little house.
Who are you?"

"I am Mr. Hare," he replied.

"Come in Mr. Hare and live with us," called the mouse and the frog.

The hare went in and settled down with the frog and the mouse in the little house.

Some time later a fox came along, and spied the little house. "That would make a fine house," he thought, and he called out:

"Little house, little house,
Who lives in the little house?"

and he heard:

"Mr. Hare, Mr. Frog, and Mr. Mouse,
We all live in the little house.
Who are you?"

"I am Mr. Fox," he replied.

"Then come in and live with us, Mr. Fox," they called back.

Mr. Fox went in and found there was just room for him too, although it was a bit of a squeeze.

The next day a bear came ambling along the road, and saw the little house. He called out:

"Little house, little house,
Who lives in the little house?"

and he heard:

"Mr. Fox, Mr. Hare, Mr. Frog, and Mr. Mouse,
We all live in the little house.
Who are you?"

"I am Mr. Bear Squash-you-all-flat," said the bear.

He then sat down on the little house, and squashed it all flat.

That was the end of the little house.

The Fisherman's Son

A long time ago, when impossible things were possible, there was a fisherman and his son. One day when the fisherman hauled in his net he found a huge gleaming red fish among the rest of his catch. For a few moments he was so excited he could only stare at it. "This fish will make me famous," he thought. "Never before has a fisherman caught such a fish."

"Stay here," he said to his son, "and look after these fish, while I go and fetch the cart to take them home."

The fisherman's son, too, was amazed by the great red fish, and while he was waiting for his father, he stroked it and started to talk to it.

"It seems a shame that a beautiful creature like you should not swim free," he said, and no sooner had he spoken than he decided to put the fish back into the sea. The great red fish slipped gratefully into the water, raised its head and spoke to the boy.

"It was kind of you to save my life. Take this bone which I have pulled from my fin. If ever you need my help, hold it up, call me, and I will come at once."

The fisherman's son placed the bone carefully in his pocket

just as his father reappeared with the cart. When the father saw that the great red fish was gone he was angry beyond belief.

"Get out of my sight," he shouted at his son, "and never let me set eyes on you again."

The boy went off sadly. He did not know where to go or what to do. In time he found himself in a great forest. He walked on and on, till suddenly he was startled by a stag rushing through the trees toward him. It was being chased by a pack of ferocious hounds followed by hunters, and it was clearly exhausted and could run no further. The boy felt sorry for the stag and took hold of its antlers as the hounds and then the hunters appeared.

"Shame on you," he said, "for chasing a tame stag. Go and find a wild beast to hunt for your sport."

The hunters, seeing the stag standing quietly by the boy, thought it must be a pet and so they turned and rode off to another part of the forest.

"It was kind of you to save my life," said the stag, and it pulled a fine brown hair from its coat. "Take this and if ever you need help, hold it out and call me. I will come at once."

The fisherman's son put the hair in his pocket with the fishbone. He thanked the stag which disappeared among the trees and wandered on once more.

As he walked he heard a strange fluttering sound overhead and, looking up, he saw a great bird – a crane – being attacked by an eagle. The crane was weak and could fight no more, and the eagle was about to kill it. The kind-hearted boy picked up a stick and threw it at the eagle, which flew off at once, fearful of this new enemy. The crane sank to the ground.

"It was kind of you to save my life," it said as it recovered its breath. "Take this feather and keep it safe. If ever you need help, hold it out and call me, and I will come."

As the fisherman's son walked on with the feather in his pocket, he met a fox running for its life, with the hounds and the huntsmen close behind. The boy just had time to hide the fox under his coat before the hounds were all around him.

"I think the fox went that way," he cried to the huntsmen, and they called off the hounds and went in the direction the boy was pointing.

"It was kind of you to save my life," said the fox. "Take this hair from my coat and keep it safe. If ever you need help, hold it out and call me. I will come at once."

The fisherman's son went on his way, and in time he reached the edge of the forest and found himself by a lovely castle.

"Who lives there?" he asked.

"A beautiful princess," he was told. "Are you one of her suitors? She plays a curious game of hide-and-seek with all who come, and says she will marry the first man who hides so well that she cannot find him."

The fisherman's son thought he would try, so boldly he went to the castle and asked to see the princess. She was indeed very

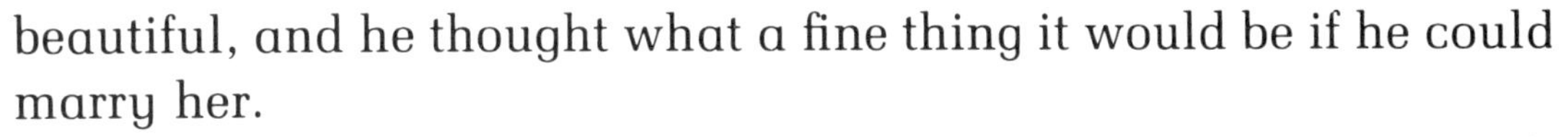

beautiful, and he thought what a fine thing it would be if he could marry her.

"Princess, I will hide where you cannot find me," he said, "but will you give me four chances?"

The princess was intrigued by this shabby boy, and agreed, thinking she would at least have some fun looking for him.

The fisherman's son went straightaway to the place where he had last seen the fish and, taking the fishbone from his pocket, he called its name.

"I am here," said the great red fish. "What can I do for you?"

"Can you take me where the princess will never find me? If you do, I shall be able to marry her."

The red fish took the boy on its back and swam deep down into the sea to some caverns where it hid him.

Now the princess had a magic mirror which she used in her games of hide-and-seek. With it she could see far and wide even through houses and hillsides. She looked in her mirror, but could not find the fisherman's son.

"What a wizard he must be," she said to herself, as she turned her mirror this way and that. Then she saw him sitting in a rocky cavern deep down in the sea and she laughed.

The next day when the boy came to the palace she smiled and said, "That was easy. You were deep down in a cavern under the sea. You will have to do better than that if you are going to marry me!"

"What an enchantress she must be," said the boy to himself, and he resolved to win this contest.

He went next to the forest and held out the stag's hair and called. When the stag came he told it that he wanted to hide and the stag took him on its back far far away to the other side of the mountains and hid him in a little cave. The stag then stood in front of the cave so that no one could see inside.

Once more the princess took out her mirror and searched far and wide for the boy. "How clever he is," she said to herself, and then the mirror picked him out hiding in the cave.

The next day she said to the boy, "Pooh! It was easy to see you in that cave."

The boy became even more determined to marry her and he set out to summon the crane. It came as soon as the boy waved the feather and called its name.

"Come with me high up into the clouds," said the crane, and took the boy on its back. All day long they hovered in the sky, while the princess searched this way and that in her mirror.

Just as she was about to give up, she spied him above her. "He is cleverer than I thought!" she said to herself.

But the next day when the boy came to the castle, she laughed and said, "You thought I would never find you among the clouds, but I spotted you easily. You only have one more chance to outwit me!"

The boy now went to the forest and, holding up the fox's hair he called the fox. When it came he explained what he wanted. "Ask her to give you fourteen days," said the fox, "and I should be able to hide you where she cannot find you."

The princess agreed, and for fourteen days the fox tunneled and dug beneath the princess's castle until it had made a hole large enough for the boy to hide in right under the princess's room. Down he went and lay there quietly. The princess took out her mirror and searched. She looked to the north, to the south, to the east, to the west; she looked high and low, round and round, and at last, exasperated, she called out:

I give up. Where are you, fisherman's son?"

"Here!" he called. "Just below you!" And he jumped out from the hole the fox had dug.

"You win, wizard," she said, and was happy to marry the fisherman's son.

He was delighted to marry such a beautiful princess. They had a great wedding in the castle, and the celebrations went on for many days.